FLO

AHSAHTA PRESS

THE NEW SERIES #41

FLOWER CART

LISA
FISHMAN

AHSAHTA PRESS

BOISE, IDAHO / 2011

Ahsahta Press, Boise State University
Boise, Idaho 83725-1525
http://ahsahtapress.boisestate.edu
http://ahsahtapress.boisestate.edu/books/fishman3/fishman3.htm

Copyright © 2011 by Lisa Fishman
Printed in the United States of America
Cover design by Quemadura; book design by Janet Holmes
First printing May 2011
ISBN-13: 978-1-934103-21-0

Library of Congress Cataloging-in-Publication Data
Fishman, Lisa, 1966–
 Flower cart / Lisa Fishman.
    p. cm. — (The new series ; #41)
ISBN-13: 978-1-934103-21-0 (pbk. : alk. paper)
ISBN-10: 1-934103-21-7 (pbk. : alk. paper)
I. Title.
PS3556.I814572F57 2011
811'.54--DC22

                         2010043825

CONTENTS

Letter from Milwaukee County School of Agriculture and Domestic Economy,
    March 10, 1916 . . . . . *3*
As it would seem *5*
Did you return to be swum *6*
Planetary in the morning *7*
Had there been a landing *8*
In which I could not say that it became a sound *10*
That was part of it *12*
Heft *13*
Herald Square: A notebook for speed and efficiency *15*
Reading *37*
Analysis *38*
"They were not to ask her questions in winter" *39*
A girl is running up a sanddune *40*
A girl had lost her house *41*
California is a lovely name *42*
Once I wrote about Mina Loy *43*
Panto *44*
the time is sick *45*
Trees I Have Seen, Copyright 1901 . . . . . *47*
Every one has a double *55*
KabbaLoom *56*
I like the acrobat by the sea *71*

About the Author *77*

FLOWER CART

F. J. SIEVERS, FARM CROPS AND SOIL FERTILITY	MILWAUKEE COUNTY SCHOOL OF AGRICULTURE AND DOMESTIC ECONOMY	I. A. MOORHEAD, ASSISTANT, FARM CROPS AND SOIL FERTILITY

F. J. SIEVERS, FARM CROPS AND SOIL
  FERTILITY
C. V. HOLSINGER, HORTICULTURE
L. M. ROEHL, FARM MECHANICS
J. J. OSTERHOUS, DAIRYING AND
  ANIMAL HUSBANDRY
C. D. ADAMS, POULTRY AND BEES
BEULAH I. COON, DOMESTIC ECONOMY
WALTER H. PERRY, ACADEMIC
  SUBJECTS
STELLA ROBBINS, MUSIC

I. A. MOORHEAD, ASSISTANT, FARM
  CROPS AND SOIL FERTILITY
B. J. PHILLIPS, ASSISTANT, FARM
  MECHANICS
HARRY D. LOCKLIN, ASSISTANT,
  HORTICULTURE
ARTHUR G. ZANDER, ASSISTANT,
  DAIRYING AND ANIMAL HUSBANDRY
HELEN M. SMITH, ASSISTANT,
  DOMESTIC ECONOMY
BRUCE BARTHOLOMEW, FARM
  ACCOUNTING AND MATHEMATICS
LILLIAN VANALSTINE, LIBRARIAN

**MILWAUKEE COUNTY SCHOOL OF AGRICULTURE
AND DOMESTIC ECONOMY**

F. J. SIEVERS, SUPERINTENDENT

OLIVE E. MANSUR, SECRETARY

WAUWATOSA, WIS.

*This is the Sample of corn
sent to me.*
C. E. M L

March 10, 1916.

Mr. C E. McLenegan,

  Public Library,

    Milwaukee, Wisconsin.

My Dear Sir:

        The sample of corn that you submitted to
me recently has been tested and its germination runs
up to 95%. From this standpoint this sample is about
up to the standard that we ordinarily require of seed
corn. On the other hand I would not advise you to
utilize this corn for seed where it is grown in any
large quantities because it seems to be entirely run
out and does not possess the characteristics of any
one particular variety. The sample submitted by you
includes a distinct mixture of at least three differ-
ent types of corn.

                Very truly yours,

                F. J. Sievers

As it would seem, to have netted
the pool around the fish knowing that
laugh just now on the hill the cart went by
water or wheel and all the noise they under
windows sing (the birds) the fish
to sleep—too many
to sort through

If there were towers
of owls over water
bodies
then chronology
fins through

I meant to ask
did you find a place
to accompany me, materia
in the hybrid form
and so became

Did you return to be swum
           across the worry line
                      a long day
to have nothing happen

"for cultivating a fine tilth"

           the sum diminishes
with each swim
and your actual emotions
vouchsafe you
           half the pool free

I was reading about pears
"to be wrapped each
in fine Writing Paper
           or spread on Wheat Straw or Moss"
meanwhile
the baby tore a paper bag a violin became

It was a red dress
I wore in the hoop house
           moreover
she chimed in

Planetary in the morning you were hazel
eyed and arms
about me, up close
rivers and leaves

erasing the list

    ~~gowns~~ Night
    Shifts
    Shirts

and the prescriptions: Greek "A" the symbol for "each" or "of each"

sure enough I dreamed of a tree house as if we were eggs or straw or a
bird or a leaf or a
branch or a horse

in the branches think of the sky

and a number of creatures we could lie down as

"rhetoric & the latter, music"

criss crossing the eyelids where we were setting out, a sea

Had there been a landing

                                  from a tipping boat

          over

              a cause

First

the pairs were not satisfied

two by _____

                      a hand taken up to touch the brow

will not stay covered

in the dusk

structure in the copper light

the chickens' necklace feathers cast

                              to dusk and clover

Had there been a leaving

            wooded

                for cover

to tree the fabric into leafing

Next

we spun around

the soul had settled out to sea   Unvacant

love of knowledge in the extra space—

the self a shore?

                                        a line of trees

In which I could not say that it became a sound

in the soggy
book of the drowned

As if you were Frank Starlight,
she my dear my part

terrain
when we brushed up against each other far away

each night I should go to bed earlier
but the traveling occurs

for which to give the local wound a name

Trish L. a scuba diver
Timi in the Beltway with her kids

The houses filled with Nightgowns
in these we find the body was

possible
beside them

Henry Vaughan, my husband is
also Henry

     makes the bread around here loudly
(hear it thumping on the table)
         when a batch is very lumpy you would know it as a cobloaf

my shooting lesson
got close to love

     I made her up
a hotdish   Instrumental

not to talk about flowers

     there's a hurry
cloud over another

dark dark dark blue on

     some kind of beginning

That was part of it
being better with two m's:
        the bird humms
beside the picture, an intricate

Was happiest lifting the cloth:
there would be breakfast
and the table under it

In the cornering
windows and doors, invisible

shade-seeking trillium
maybe remember

The vernacular is a form of plantlife
A wooden egg
in a sun-square house
the piano where it is creates

So important has the floor
become, the pine trees
holding everything up

Heft

     and hue

to have unheld a scale—

silver dishes little mirrors on their chains—

they go that way, This

     and hoist

It's not like looking into a pool,

to let your intelligence run away with you

Come back quarter size, apricot moon

A changeling is a child who

appeared under cover

of the ordinary, in exchange

the morning came

     I have such pretty handwriting

     no one said but I myself thought it

     to myself so I matted it

     like the grasses or a canvas or some

     uncombed hair. It became a mess

     which was the research of where things go.

A child could figure it out
if there is such a thing as "out"
in the sense of being figured in

The thinking was like Origami,
everyone folded out of birds, into specific
kinds of birds
      I call you

          hickory

          category

          dot

HERALD SQUARE

REG. U. S. PAT. OFFICE

A notebook for speed and efficiency... the leaves turn swiftly and lie flat... the book will stand alone for transcribing...

15-R-HG-620

Book No._____ From_____ to_____

12 inches in 1 foot

May Day – 1st day of May

This is 5th day of week and month.

recipe calls for 8 oz or 1 cup

910 Pearl St.

I bought some fuchsia colored pillows

for the studio couch

I put some cucumbers in the salad.

my husband came back for his umbrella

when he saw the thunder clouds.

I asked
my brother to get me ^ bubblebath at the drugstore.
                  some

                               my neighbors said

                               they would drop by

                               later. Please state

                               your name and age.

1. 9 doz cookies	1 – 7 rolls of wallpaper
2. gained 2 lbs. today	2 – exits in ^ house
3. 18 for supper	3. 7 grandchildren
4. 25 sentences	4. 2:30
5. there are 356 days	5. 3 windows

17

Franklin got a
job at the factory
in January.
Please write the
word satellite on the
blackboard.

1. – 6 pack of beer
2. – 12 hours of sleep.
3. – 7 people
4. – 50 hostages in Iran
5. –1.50 for 5 lbs
6. – 9:35 am:

cart, card, guard
park, bark
harm, harp

It won't do any harm to
have some pie ala mode.
Father likes to sit in the armchair.

The children decided to play leap frog.
What do you plan to do in the meantime.
Either of them will eat sea food.

decide, beside, design
real estate
beehive
peaceful
neither

major operation

paper clip

beach umbrella

medium rare

who is at bat?

pat on the back

peanut brittle

my, oh, my

boil over

I gave him some goldfish for his
birthday. I have to get some clothespins
and doughnuts from the grocery store.

I wish I could go to the ballgame.
I "   " stay home from school.
I "   " wear long? trousers
I "   " drive a car.
I "   " some cheese to eat

I still wash my hands with soap.
I "   " teeth before breakfast.
I "   " brush my hair before I come downstairs.

I am not making any noise
I am telling you the truth
I am going to

I never knew Father?

waffle iron
follow-up
document
tom boy
solitary
blossom

I bought the fuchsia colored pillows
for the studio couch. He tried to get the
tuba and music box in the suitcase.
I put some cucumbers in the salad.

runway
number
lumber yard
judgment
husband
gun powder
fun house
trumpet
double talk

My husband came back for his umbrella
when he saw the thunder cloud. I asked
my brother to get me some bubble bath
from the drug store. Would you like
some pumpkin pie?

daughter
caution
saucepan
because

pawn shop
laundry
jaw breaker
thoughtful
fraudulent
flawless
awful

thought, thawed,
caught, gone
gauze, cause

I put some walnuts in the cookies.
He bought some jawbreakers for the
children. He brought over a wrench to
fix the faucet in the laundry tub. I feel awful
because I can't remember the authors name.

You promised to fix the waffle iron
for me. We had chop suey for
dinner. My god mother lives in
Montana.

truthful

tooth pick

soup bowl

plumage

moonlight

loophole

juke box

hoof print

gooseberries

fruitcake

foolish

fluid drive

do you have any soup bones?

I think that is a foolish question.

mount, mound

bound and pound.

cloud and clown.

counterfeit

cloudburst

Brownies

boundary

downtown, noun,

doubt.

1. You will find some brownies and
2. They laid the foundation for the house
   on ground hogs day.

1. 800 series number
2.
3. $46.00   14.00
4. Boat ride—enjoyed it much.
5. 49 people at picnic, 4 doz. ears of corn.
6. Sig. is a nice person to put up with us.

paper

pilot

beach, peach,

my, pie buy, by bye

Miami

1. 780 numbers

2.   fell

3. 2 ft snow ^ Minnesota

4. 60 days to 1st day of

5.

6. program about leprosy

November first

tapioca pudding

tower of London

darn the socks

doughnuts and coffee,

daughter

neighbor

nineteen

table manners

Where have you been?

When are you leaving?

Why did you come?

What do you want?

What did you buy?

Why are you _____ X

When is your birthday?

Please tell me why you are leaving

What did you buy?

What did you say?

Why didn't you answer my letter?

To whom are you speaking?

Why don't you sew in the morning?

drape
draft
dream

drown
drive
drove

4-19-1979

record player
question mark
elevator

be at center at 1:00 oclock

1.) 5
2.) 399-6407
3.) 85.00
4.) 2 sis + 1 brother
5.) 6 chicks
6.) 7 grandchildren

1. Main 1222

2. 5,280

3. no 2 lead pencil

4. 3:45

5. $25.00

6. size 7 1/2 AA

7. 1 cube ft.

8. March 20 1st day

        of spring

rent 225. a month

17 inches from the floor

13 x 13 x 10

4″ snow 60 degrees

$148 gas bill

2 new cars.

2:30

score was 120

2 - toes

17″ from the floor

2 stomachs

60 people

12 yrs old

1,000 legs

11-8-79

—was missing

April 3 Monday

40 employees

7-14-1965

1000's of eggs

4 to go

5 peppers

9,800 hairs

The boyscout picnic was spoiled by
poison ivy. You have a choice of oyster
or lobster.

Do you have a fall wardrobe

Do you own a black dress?

Have you got your fall house cleaning?

summer

Tuesday

Thursday

winter

yesterday

Wednesday

tomorrow

today

tonight

I must wash the woodwork today.

Do you have anything I can use

for a book mark?

tooth extracted ↑

tooth separated ||

" filled O

" absent t

" on plate ∩

artificial crown P

tooth on bridge A

tooth regulated ⅋

abcess treated Δ

inlay □

80th day in 1980
286 days left in year

7000 employees laid off

handiman
654 – 7455
Don Archambeau

Reading

A number of transitional objects
starting with one
may be meant.

There are certain things I don't mean.

What a pleasure to say.

A pattern in four parts?
Loft, bed in the loft,
a float,
pool. He was her
favorite boat, he mothered
her.
I want to shoot the birds
she sometimes thought.

There is so much that happens
in the little words.

Analysis

It was the hidden quality of genitals
originally compared, in a reworking of Winnicott
one told to you. Then the quotation could enter
zero as a great
divide. But I would like to be here, not her
average cadabra loom. And the mouse was as big as the girl
the doctor knew. How to convey
that precisely, how sure
to be a color rinsed the vine or what
your hands were stained with coming true.

"They were not to ask her questions in winter"
even ecstatic
going down the slide. Out of

a self a like
condition:

Askesis is the opposite of going out
Did we ever talk about math?
someone I didn't know once

if you rearrange it like that. As, in, an
elevator up up up will not chime shut
Mercutia

A girl is running up a sanddune,

down the other side

into a lake

There are? clouds over the moon,

a cloudy night (~~for it is night~~)

A girl had lost her house

in Minnesota

when a tornado leveled a town

There was nothing to sew in the thriftshop

turned on its corner like a washing machine

went for a ride

and the sand under the girl's feet as she runs

California is a lovely name

she thought, thinking of quietly

shined up moon

Once I wrote about Mina Loy (to show you a motorcycle)

I grew up on / a trampoline

pitched like a tent in the mangoes (a shoe and a dress)

full of water, some summer / possible only

under the nail (a situation such as love) & set the U-shaped slinky

to uncoil down the stairs / find I partly

agog in the universe, Mister Flyspeck

in the poppies, where a house

I lived in once

Panto

The pool was covered by a sheath of leaves

There was Invisible again, wearing the sign

Off in the distance

was a way of placing the poplars

I said that I wanted to mean

you could stay

here as my vocabulary, o you could

materialize among the notes

on grapes, a clustered emphasis

the hill makes

mouth to ear or a gesture

tensing its legs

the time is sick and

if everything was once alive, had been alive

the author could wear

the unraked leaves   a crown of peas

or whirl around the other other

            out of joynt

My big black coat

was found in the kitchen

beside the jar of oats   A mystery

starts at 9

she likes that

spun self coil

the tree came down beside

TREES·I·HAVE
SEEN

Copyright, 1901,
by
DODD, MEAD & COMPANY

First edition, May, 1901

Name and address of the owner of this Book, and
the date when it was acquired.

———————

Name

Residence

Date

PREFACE

THIS little book is designed to be used with your "How to Know the Trees," "Our Native Trees," etc. It is not always convenient to bring your book to the tree, it is not always possible to bring the tree to your book; but when in your walks you see an unfamiliar tree jot down your impressions of it in this book. Then at your leisure you can verify your observations with the aid of the larger book.

Trees I Have Seen

A SAMPLE PAGE

Date—*June 23, 1900.*

Where seen—*Lenox, Mass.*

Characteristics of the locality—*Sparsely timbered, near river bank ; rich soil.*

The bark—*Ashy gray, flaky.*

The branches—*Pendulous, light green when young, not corky. Note : Young shoots of Rock Elm, a tree which greatly resembles this, are marked lengthwise with many corky ridges.*

The leaves—

How grouped—*Singly.*

Size—*2 to 5 inches long, 1½ to 2½ wide. Note: Leaves of Slippery Elm are twice as large.*

Shape—*Oval, with tapering apex and rounded or slightly pointed base. The two sides are not uniform.*

Margin—*Serrated.*

How veined—*Veins straight and conspicuous, running off from main rib.*

Remarks : *Leaf is smooth on upper side, roughish on the under side.*

Trees I Have Seen

A SAMPLE PAGE

Flower—*Not visible. Note : This tree blossoms in March and April.*

Fruit—*Not visible. Note: Seedtime is the last of May.*

Common and scientific names—*American Elm, White Elm, Ulmus Americana.*

Family—*Elm.*

Remarks—*A beautiful tree, with its trim trunk, broad round head, and pendulous branches. It is no dwarf either, as it sometimes attains a height of one hundred feet and a girth of twenty feet. A striking feature is the enormous number of leaves, which on a large elm often reaches several millions. The wood is hard, as witness Dr. Holmes in "The One-Hoss Shay"—*

"The hubs of logs from the 'Settler's Ellum',—
Last of its timber,—they couldn't sell 'em,
Never an axe had seen their chips,
And the wedges flew from between their lips
Their blunt ends frizzled like celery tips."

Trees I Have Seen

Date— March 5 - 1910

Where seen— Campus and River Bottoms

Characteristics of the locality— Gregarious - mesophytic - Sandy Hillsides or wet river bottom land.

The bark— Twigs - dark brown - smooth
Trunk - ashy gray - possessof - scaly surface

The branches— long - slender, drooping - terete.
{Pendulous}

The leaves—

How grouped—

Size—

Shape—

Margin—

How veined—

Trees I Have Seen

Flower—

Fruit—

Common and scientific names *Ulmus americana*
White or water elm

Family— *Urticaceae* - Elms, Huck berry
Plane tree, Hemp, Hop, osage orange
Remarks: mulberry- nettles.

Buds - Lateral flower and leaf -
Terminal. 0. $\frac{1}{8}$ - $\frac{1}{4}$ in
Phyllotaxy $\frac{1}{2}$.
ovate, acute, glabrous, flattened.
Scales chestnut brown, indurated
glabrous.

Leaf Scars - Semi- orbicular circular, smooth.

lf. traces - 3± sub. lunate

Lenticels - scattered - elliptical -

6   Trees I Have Seen

Date— *March 5. 1910*

Where seen— *Campus*

Characteristics of the locality— *Gregarious-
mesophytic.*

The bark— *Dark-reddish brown- Shallow fissured-flat scales
Stiff-more erect han americana*

The branches— *Stout- green to light brown- pubescent-
lenticels small ∞.*

The leaves—

How grouped—

Size—

Shape—

Margin—

How veined —

Trees I Have Seen

7

Flower—

Fruit—

Common and scientific names *Ulmus Fulva or Pubescens*
Red or Slippery Elm
Family— *Utricaceae. nettle*

Remarks:

Buds.
Ovate, obtuse, rounded - rusty hairy.

8 Trees I Have Seen

Date— March 5, 1910

Where seen— Avenue - Mr Fiske's yard, - front -

Characteristics of the locality—

The bark—

The branches— Rough winged -

The leaves—

How grouped—

Size—

Shape—

Margin—

How veined—

Trees I Have Seen

Flower—

Fruit—

Common and scientific names *Ulmus alata.*
Winged Elm.

Family—

Remarks:

Trees I Have Seen

Date—

Where seen— *Habit -*

   Characteristics of the locality—

The bark—

The branches—

~~The leaves~~ *Buds*

   How grouped—   *Figure P. 320 model*

   Size—

   Shape—

   Margin—

   How veined—

Lz of Diagram

Trees I Have Seen

Flower—

Fruit—

Common and scientific names

Family—

Remarks:

Flower —

Floral Plan

Fruit.

Floral Parts
ovary re

Every one has a double

Through the ridges in the stem

Yet not fluted

      Or the color of the bark

to be likened to a person's eye, a rather

beautiful one's eye, because right here

the sun came in

      (these oval shadows on the page)

(they move when I move the page)

KabbaLoom

Material	mater	matrix	womb	(check oed)
linen			line	
ribbon			rib	
cloth	hotel			
lace	like			
border			border	
needle	ladder			
hem			edge	
crease			erase	
fold			fold	
cloth	clock	time	clot	
wool			o, o	
loom			loam	
pin			loop	

63

shine: neige

shine: hinge

shine: s/he, i

                          n   new

snow: cloth

hotel: hymn

hem   me

          h   hinge

H   (ladders, arm across)
          (arms, ladder across)

a run through

if letters can house a word

then words are not made of letters but letters are made of words

a shape makes a letter   a body

                                        ladders,
                                        arms

alternatives / argument

if sound is a body of

sounds (housed)

then, new

if

                                        one to another through

not Language

not Object

        materia   mater(ia)

                i, a (mater / mother)

    whose rib floats, ribbon-

    like

women sewing

the text Isle

the fabric I ate

and ate

because I do not sew

                              any fold

what is even a fold

a book is
                    felled

without a fold a book is a page

or a cloth

                    linen?   line   n

                                        (a kneeling)

              clot   h

                                    (a kneeling *at*)

—just trying to see the shapes, to see inside

a letter

being made of words

sometimes you can hear   the shapes

sometimes a shape is a wall

Do not kneel

at it

Love

can be too many voices, so to undo

the loop, like a pin

        drop

           so to hear

can be sculptural

Here is a square

room with a line in it

              o, o

        I unhooked these from the wool
        border
        in order   to hear

        out

in which the square became a circle

and returned to the room

we stepped out of, as in the Marriage

of Figaro, midsummer dream

of the etymon, a comedy, Keats

might have known

a margin is a laughter, lording

around / not over

the page   niege   new

preferring the fig

leaves like genitals

preferring the mint

flagrant, all over the field

and right here, where Jack the cat is sitting

about to roll

we have the sun on us and a sentence

we have the hotel and the loam

        o, tell   o, am

                        sewn a fabulous wingspan

                        on the numberblades, a many

                        body shone

ribbed,

bode

I like the acrobat by the sea. He chose not to include it.

Well sometimes an object may be put to use. May be used to put together other things such as a very long walk through a small room, the smallest room in a person's face looking out at where the tree is not. The tree was cut down by the city after one branch broke in a storm. The tree was gigantic.

This could continue only by being a letter because what is most real is the person in the alcove or the object on the table or the shimmering idea. Could you repeat that, with a different emphasis, and if so is the distance altered while votes are counted, for today is Tuesday Nov. 2 2010; bass thumping through apartment wall sounds Republican and one is afraid. At 11:04 abandon this.

Begin again, third day, eleventh month. In a tunnel called after the lavender gatherer in a field in the sud-ouest where a box was found—familiar elements. Blue ink as blue as poppies because this is all one thing, might be known as the future of which there is, literally, no such thing. If there were, it would mean it had already happened. Hi again. Correction: it would mean it is happening now, is just this, and the past is this too. I would do almost anything to know.

But have to scale back my ambitions: wish to decipher the small handwriting in the notebook with 8 legs—for the book of notes is simultaneously an insect; one returns to Aristotle's invention of the word insect based on the body in sections. Then the sidereal comes into play because I'm unsure of that word and perhaps something could happen there. About seeing, or about thirst, excluding the rural and the natatorium with built-in stars, except I loved it—the pool built in to the mountain in Salt Lake—so it has to change.

You were going there too, right? Everybody's parents are here in the room, what should we do with them? All the ghosts ahead of time together in the present relation, confused about the others and the others. I thought so in science, with caution. What would happen if it just opened? On the moon, there must be graffiti along with trash, so along with the notebook being written in beside me, not by me, on the train or bus in the traveling room, I might be able to think about that.

ACKNOWLEDGMENTS

Thanks to the editors who first published the following poems and portions, some of which have been revised, retitled, or recombined since. *Bird Dog:* "Did you return to be swum," "Planetary in the morning," "Had there been a landing"; *Interim:* "In which I could not say that it became a sound"; *1913 a journal of forms:* "Heft"; *Conduit:* from "Herald Square: A notebook for speed and efficiency"; *mtd:* "Reading," "Analysis," "They were not to ask her questions in winter"; *No Tell Motel:* "As it would seem," "A girl is running up a sanddune," "A girl had lost her house," "California is a lovely name"; *Volt:* "Once I wrote about Mina Loy" (as "Salzburg, a Lecture"); *Women's Studies Quarterly:* "the time is sick" (as "Influence"). "Heft" also appears on the Poetry Foundation's website. "KabbaLoom" was first published as a chapbook by Wyrd Press (Boulder, 2007); my thanks to Abbey Pleviak.

I thank Bridget Lowe for "Letter from Milwaukee County School of Agriculture and Domestic Economy, March 10, 1916" and "Herald Square: A notebook for speed and efficiency"—both of which she found in a thrift shop in southern Wisconsin and gave to me. The contents of "Herald Square" are transcribed from that notebook, with many additional pages omitted for reasons of space.

I thank Richard Meier for *Trees I Have Seen,* Copyright 1901. He found the small book with handwritten notes and illustrations in a cardboard box full of onion skins in a barn in southern Wisconsin and gave it to me.

For the hoop house, the pears to be wrapped in fine Writing Paper, the notes on grapes, the material and immaterial forms of cultivation from which everything emerges, I thank Henry James Morren.

ABOUT THE AUTHOR

LISA FISHMAN lives in Orfordville and Madison, Wisconsin, and commutes to Columbia College Chicago, where she teaches poetry and literature.

ALSO BY LISA FISHMAN

BOOKS

Current (Parlor Press, 2010)
The Happiness Experiment (Ahsahta, 2007)
Dear, Read (Ahsahta, 2002)
The Deep Heart's Core Is a Suitcase (New Issues Press, 1996)

CHAPBOOKS

at the same time as scattering (Albion Books, 2010)
Lining (Boxwood Editions, 2009)
'The Holy Spirit does not deal in synonimes': Elizabeth Barrett's Marginalia in the Margins of Her Greek and Hebrew Bibles (Parlor Press, 2007)
Kabbaloom (Wyrd Press, 2008)

Ahsahta Press

SAWTOOTH POETRY PRIZE SERIES

2002: Aaron McCollough, *Welkin* (Brenda Hillman, judge)
2003: Graham Foust, *Leave the Room to Itself* (Joe Wenderoth, judge)
2004: Noah Eli Gordon, *The Area of Sound Called the Subtone* (Claudia Rankine, judge)
2005: Karla Kelsey, *Knowledge, Forms, The Aviary* (Carolyn Forché, judge)
2006: Paige Ackerson-Kiely, *In No One's Land* (D. A. Powell, judge)
2007: Rusty Morrison, *the true keeps calm biding its story* (Peter Gizzi, judge)
2008: Barbara Maloutas, *the whole Marie* (C. D. Wright, judge)
2009: Julie Carr, *100 Notes on Violence* (Rae Armantrout, judge)
2010: James Meetze, *Dayglo* (Terrance Hayes, judge)

Ahsahta Press is committed to preserving ancient forests and natural resources. We elected to print this title on 30% post-consumer recycled paper, processed chlorine-free. As a result, we have saved:

1 Tree (40' tall and 6-8" diameter)
1 Million BTUs of Total Energy
135 Pounds of Greenhouse Gases
649 Gallons of Wastewater
39 Pounds of Solid Waste

Ahsahta Press made this paper choice because our printer, Thomson-Shore, Inc., is a member of Green Press Initiative, a nonprofit program dedicated to supporting authors, publishers, and suppliers in their efforts to reduce their use of fiber obtained from endangered forests.

For more information, visit www.greenpressinitiative.org

Environmental impact estimates were made using the Environmental Defense Paper Calculator. For more information visit: www.edf.org/papercalculator

Ahsahta Press

NEW SERIES

1. Lance Phillips, *Corpus Socius*
2. Heather Sellers, *Drinking Girls and Their Dresses*
3. Lisa Fishman, *Dear, Read*
4. Peggy Hamilton, *Forbidden City*
5. Dan Beachy-Quick, *Spell*
6. Liz Waldner, *Saving the Appearances*
7. Charles O. Hartman, *Island*
8. Lance Phillips, *Cur aliquid vidi*
9. Sandra Miller, *oriflamme.*
10. Brigitte Byrd, *Fence Above the Sea*
11. Ethan Paquin, *The Violence*
12. Ed Allen, *67 Mixed Messages*
13. Brian Henry, *Quarantine*
14. Kate Greenstreet, *case sensitive*
15. Aaron McCollough, *Little Ease*
16. Susan Tichy, *Bone Pagoda*
17. Susan Briante, *Pioneers in the Study of Motion*
18. Lisa Fishman, *The Happiness Experiment*
19. Heidi Lynn Staples, *Dog Girl*
20. David Mutschlecner, *Sign*
21. Kristi Maxwell, *Realm Sixty-four*
22. G. E. Patterson, *To and From*
23. Chris Vitiello, *Irresponsibility*
24. Stephanie Strickland, *Zone : Zero*
25. Charles O. Hartman, *New and Selected Poems*
26. Kathleen Jesme, *The Plum-Stone Game*
27. Ben Doller, *FAQ:*
28. Carrie Olivia Adams, *Intervening Absence*
29. Rachel Loden, *Dick of the Dead*
30. Brigitte Byrd, *Song of a Living Room*
31. Kate Greenstreet, *The Last 4 Things*
32. Brenda Iijima, *If Not Metamorphic*
33. Sandra Doller, *Chora.*
34. Susan Tichy, *Gallowglass*
35. Lance Phillips, *These Indicium Tales*
36. Karla Kelsey, *Iteration Nets*
37. Brian Teare, *Pleasure*
38. Kirsten Kaschock, *A Beautiful Name for a Girl*
39. Susan Briante, *Utopia Minus*
40. Brian Henry, *Lessness*
41. Lisa Fishman, *Flower Cart*

This book is set in Apollo MT type with Impact display titles
by Ahsahta Press at Boise State University
and printed by Thomson-Shore, Inc.
Cover design by Quemadura.
Book design by Janet Holmes.

AHSAHTA PRESS

2011

JANET HOLMES, DIRECTOR

KAT COE

CHRIS CRAWFORD

TIMOTHY DAVIS

CHARLES GABEL

KATE HOLLAND

GENNA KOHLHARDT

BREONNA KRAFFT

MATT TRUSLOW

ZACH VESPER

EVAN WESTERFIELD